You can read this way up!

OWL BAT
BAT OWL

Marie-Louise Fitzpatrick

Or ... you can read this way up!

WALKER BOOKS
AND SUBSIDIARIES
LONDON · BOSTON · SYDNEY · AUCKLAND

For Michael, because it all began with him. xxx

First published 2016 by Walker Books Ltd, 87 Vauxhall Walk, London SE11 5HJ • This edition published 2018 • © 2016 Marie-Louise Fitzpatrick • 10 9 8 7 6 5 4 3 2 1
The right of Marie-Louise Fitzpatrick to be identified as author of this work has been asserted in accordance with the Copyright, Designs and Patents Act 1988
This book has been typeset in Intro • Printed in China • All rights reserved. No part of this book may be reproduced, transmitted or stored in an information retrieval system in any form or by any means, graphic, electronic or mechanical, including photocopying, taping and recording, without prior written permission from the publisher.
British Library Cataloguing in Publication Data: a catalogue record for this book is available from the British Library • ISBN 978-1-4063-7344-8 • www.walker.co.uk